Baboon on the Moon

PHASE 3 AND 4

/oo/

Level 4 – Blue

Helpful Hints for Reading at Home

The graphemes (written letters) and phonemes (units of sound) used throughout this series are aligned with Letters and Sounds. This offers a consistent approach to learning whether reading at home or in the classroom.

HERE IS A LIST OF NEW PHONEMES FOR THIS PHASE OF LEARNING. AN EXAMPLE OF THE PRONUNCIATION CAN BE FOUND IN BRACKETS.

Phase 3			
j (jug)	v (van)	w (wet)	x (fox)
y (yellow)	z (zoo)	zz (buzz)	qu (quick)
ch (chip)	sh (shop)	th (thin/then)	ng (ring)
ai (rain)	ee (feet)	igh (night)	oa (boat)
oo (boot/look)	ar (farm)	or (for)	ur (hurt)
ow (cow)	oi (coin)	ear (dear)	air (fair)
ure (sure)	er (corner)		

HERE ARE SOME WORDS WHICH YOUR CHILD MAY FIND TRICKY.

Phase 3 Tricky Words			
he	you	she	they
we	all	me	are
be	my	was	her

Phase 4 Tricky Words			
said	were	have	there
like	little	so	one
do	when	some	out
come	what		

TOP TIPS FOR HELPING YOUR CHILD TO READ:

• Allow children time to break down unfamiliar words into units of sound and then encourage children to string these sounds together to create the word.

• Encourage your child to point out any focus phonics when they are used.

• Read through the book more than once to grow confidence.

• Ask simple questions about the text to assess understanding.

• Encourage children to use illustrations as prompts.

PHASE 3 AND 4
/oo/

This book focuses on the phoneme /oo/ and is a blue level 4 book band.

Baboon on the Moon

Written by
Emilie Dufresne

Illustrated by
Richard Bayley

"The zoo is missing a baboon. We need you to look for the baboon!"

"Mum, we need to help look for the baboon too!" said Oona.

Mum shook Oona's hand. "We will get that baboon back in the zoo!"

"Mum, look! The baboon took my Food Loops!" said Oona.

But Mum said, "Oona, Food Loops are not for baboons! Pick up that mess."

Mum said, "Oona, I need the book to put it back."

"But Mum, the baboon took my book!"
Oona said with a moan.
"No, look, that is the book," said Mum.

"Put on the hat," Mum said to Oona.
"You need to get in the pool."

"But Mum, Baboon took my hat and got in the pool!" Oona said.

"Goodness me, look at this mess! Can you fix this, Oona?" said Mum.

"Mum, look quick! Baboon is in my room!
No, do not poo, Baboon!"

Mum said, "We need to go soon. Pick up the bassoon, Oona!"

"Mum! Baboon has got my bassoon. Baboon, get back!" Oona said, in a mood.

"Oona, look at the rain. Get the rain mac off the hook," said Mum.

"But Mum, Baboon's in my hood!" said Oona. She shook her rain mac to get rid of Baboon.

"Oona, it is noon! We need to meet Soo in the woods for a picnic," said Mum.

"Oona, can I get a scoop?" said Soo.
"Can we get a scoop for Soo – Baboon,
no!" said Oona.

"Oona, look at the mess. Now the scoop is on Soo... Can you be good?" said Mum.

"But Mum, the baboon did a hop and sent the scoop right into Soo!" Oona said.

"Look, Baboon, this is not cool. Now I look a fool," said Oona to the baboon.

The baboon was in a mood. He did a huff and a puff. Baboon was sad.

"Oona, look. Is it the baboon on the moon? Is he in a mood?"

"Mum, we need to ring the zoo and get Baboon off the moon!" said Oona.

"The baboon is back in the zoo. Good job, Oona," said Mum.

"I miss Baboon," said Oona.
"But Baboon took the food, book, hat
and bassoon..." said Mum.

"Baboon, we got you a scoop! You do not need to be in a mood!" said Oona.

Baboon on the Moon

1. What food did the baboon steal from Oona?

2. What musical instrument did the baboon steal from Oona?

   (a)   A drum

   (b)   A bassoon

   (c)   A guitar

3. How do you think Oona was feeling when the baboon was getting her in trouble with Mum?

4. What did Oona do to make the baboon less moody?

5. What would you have done with the baboon if you were Oona?

©This edition published in 2021.
First published in 2020.
BookLife Publishing Ltd.
King's Lynn, Norfolk PE30 4LS

ISBN 978-1-83927-290-5

All rights reserved. Printed in Malta.
A catalogue record for this book is available from
the British Library.

Baboon on the Moon
Written by Emilie Dufresne
Illustrated by Richard Bayley

An Introduction to BookLife Readers...

Our Readers have been specifically created in line with the London Institute of Education's approach to book banding and are phonetically decodable and ordered to support each phase of the Letters and Sounds document.

Each book has been created to provide the best possible reading and learning experience. Our aim is to share our love of books with children, providing both emerging readers and prolific page-turners with beautiful books that are guaranteed to provoke interest and learning, regardless of ability.

BOOK BAND GRADED using the Institute of Education's approach to levelling.

PHONETICALLY DECODABLE supporting each phase of Letters and Sounds.

EXERCISES AND QUESTIONS to offer reinforcement and to ascertain comprehension.

BEAUTIFULLY ILLUSTRATED to inspire and provoke engagement, providing a variety of styles for the reader to enjoy whilst reading through the series.

AUTHOR INSIGHT:
EMILIE DUFRESNE

Born in Québec, Canada, Emilie Dufresne's academic achievements explain the knowledge and creativity that can be found in her books. At a young age, she received the award of Norfolk County Scholar, recognising her top grades in school. At the University of Kent, Emilie obtained a First Class Honours degree in English and American Literature, and was awarded a Masters in The Contemporary with Distinction. She has published over 60 books with BookLife Publishing, in subjects ranging from science to geography, art and sports, and even animals as superheroes! Children enjoy Emilie's books because of the detailed narrative and the engaging way she writes, which always entices children to want to learn more.

PHASE 3 AND 4
/oo/

This book focuses on the phoneme /oo/ and is a blue level 4 book band.